Mehndi Boy

By Zain Bandali

Illustrated by Jani Balakumar

annick press

toronto · berkeley

To all the boys who never got to try on mehndi.
—Z.B.

To my supportive family, whose words of
encouragement helped me along the way.
—J.B.

Facts in the "Did You Know?" section (p. 98–99) were
sourced from the author's family and community, and
from the following sources:

https://madainproject.com/ramesses_ii_mummy

https://www.britannica.com/plant/henna

Henna's Secret History: The History, Mystery & Folklore of Henna
by Marie Anakee Miczak (Writers Club Press, 2001)

https://people.howstuffworks.com/culture-traditions/body-art/
henna-tattoo.htm

https://www.encyclopedia.com/science-and-technology/chemistry/
organic-chemistry/henna

https://en.wikipedia.org/wiki/Henna#cite_note-5

https://www.vogue.in/content/the-history-of-bridal-mehandi-
how-the-tradition-came-to-be

https://www.hindustantimes.com/trending/instead-of-groom-
s-name-bride-hides-famous-paintings-in-wedding-mehendi-
watch-101657187903719.html

We acknowledge the support of the Canada Council for the Arts and the Ontario Arts Council, and the participation of
the Government of Canada/la participation du gouvernement du Canada for our publishing activities.

Library and Archives Canada Cataloguing in Publication
Title: Mehndi boy / written by Zain Bandali ; illustrated by Jani Balakumar.
Names: Bandali, Zain, author. | Balakumar, Jani, illustrator.
Identifiers: Canadiana (print) 20230160301 | Canadiana (ebook)
2023016031X | ISBN 9781773217925 (hardcover) | ISBN 9781773217949
(HTML) | ISBN 9781773217956 (PDF)
Classification: LCC PS8603.A618 M46 2023 | DDC jC813/.6,Äîdc23

Published in the U.S.A. by Annick Press (U.S.) Ltd.
Distributed in Canada by University of Toronto Press.
Distributed in the U.S.A. by Publishers Group West.

Printed in China

annickpress.com

Also available as an e-book. Please visit annickpress.com/ebooks for more details.

Table of Contents

Chapter 1

*C*hickadee-dee-dee-dee . . .

"I am *not* ready to wake up!" Tehzeeb groaned as he pulled a pillow over his head. But he could still hear the chickadees merrily singing from the birdhouse outside his window.

Tehzeeb tried to go back to his dream. He'd been

dreaming about weddings for the past few nights—of all the celebrations he'd been to, he loved weddings the most. In this one, he was wearing a royal blue kurta with a white shawl and pearls around his neck. All the guests were staring at him in awe. The special outfit made him feel like the most dazzling version of himself.

Chickadee-dee-dee-dee . . .

Chickadee-dee-dee-dee . . .

He pictured the fancy decorations, the glittering gold jewelry, the fresh marigolds and roses, the delicious buffet food, and the bride's mehndi . . .

Chickadee-dee-dee-dee . . .

Chickadee-dee—

"Tez!" came a loud screech from downstairs.

Tehzeeb opened his eyes.

"Wakey wakey! I hope you remembered what today is," his mother called from the kitchen. "Tehzeeb!"

Tehzeeb leapt out of bed—how could he forget? He couldn't sleep in this weekend, dreaming about weddings. Today was Navroz, the very first day of spring.

When Tehzeeb marched into the kitchen, he found his mom cooking up a storm.

He smelled the spicy scent of cardamom and the sugary sweetness of doughnuts. Bollywood tunes were blasting through the room. His mom swayed to the beat while stirring the batter.

"Ya Ali Madad, Mommy. Oh, and Navroz Mubarak!" said Tehzeeb with a giant smile.

"Mawla Ali Madad and Navroz Mubarak, Tehzeeb beta," she said. "Help yourself, sleepyhead." He grabbed a freshly fried doughnut shaped like a triangle off the cooling rack.

"Mmmm, mandazi—my favorite!"

"Yes, beta, I am making mandazi and channa bateta for the party this afternoon." She beamed as she dropped more mandazi into the frying oil.

Each Navroz, Tehzeeb's family would head over to Ayaz Uncle's house to celebrate the beginning of the new year. Since his family moved from India to Tanzania a few generations ago, his relatives would cook all the tastiest Swahili, Gujarati and Kutchi delicacies to share.

Ayaz Uncle was his favorite relative since he always brought Tehzeeb the most unique souvenirs and trinkets from his travels around the world. He loved making art as much as Tehzeeb, too. His daughter, Rahima, was like a big sister to Tehzeeb even though they were first cousins. She wore the prettiest outfits and always shared her old scarves, belts, and jewelry with him when she got tired of them. Tehzeeb didn't mind—he loved Rahima's hand-me-downs.

"Make sure to wear something special and *don't forget to do your brush*," his mom said, pretending to brush her teeth with a spatula.

Tehzeeb couldn't contain his excitement. He popped another mandazi in his mouth then galloped upstairs to get ready. He already knew just what he wanted to wear—the kanzu Ayaz Uncle brought him from Zanzibar last month. The kanzu was gold like the Serengeti grasslands and made Tehzeeb feel like royalty.

Once he'd put on the kanzu and matching topi, he was almost ready. He just needed to pack his bag for the hour-long drive. He grabbed his sketchbook, pencil crayons, and, last but certainly not least, his stuffie, Mr. Unicorn.

He was so excited that he almost forgot his mom's reminder. With just two minutes to spare, Tehzeeb ran to the washroom to brush quickly and make sure he had no mandazi crumbs stuck between his teeth. Royal princes needed to have a sparkling smile, after all!

Chapter 2

In the car, Tehzeeb decided to draw a Navroz card for Ayaz Uncle. He drew the traditional wheatgrass, roji, tied with a ruby-red ribbon. He decorated the card with tall tulips, rainbow-colored eggs, and spring bumblebees buzzing all around. He couldn't wait to show Ayaz Uncle.

When they arrived, Ayaz Uncle's house was decked with fairy lights twinkling above the bricks, colorful streamers hugging the porch columns, and dozens of balloons on either side of the front door. *This seems different*, thought Tehzeeb. As much as Ayaz Uncle and Rahima loved to decorate for Navroz, *this* seemed a bit over the top. What was going on?

Tehzeeb's parents looked puzzled, too. He followed them across the front yard. Before they could even knock, the door swung open. Ayaz Uncle grinned at them, his arms spread wide.

"Acho, acho! Andar acho! Come in, everyone. Navroz Mubarak!"

Suddenly, Tehzeeb noticed a banner behind Ayaz Uncle that said *Congratulations, Rahima and Karim!*

His mom noticed it, too. "Mubaraki, Ayaz Bha!" she exclaimed. "Our Rahima finally got engaged?"

Tehzeeb's jaw dropped. No wonder he'd been dreaming of weddings—maybe that was the universe's way of telling him his favorite cousin had gotten engaged!

"Yes, it happened a couple of days ago," Ayaz Uncle said. "We thought it would be so special to mark Karim's proposal at our Navroz gathering."

"It's a dream come true!" squealed Tehzeeb as he gave Ayaz Uncle a big hug.

"Wow, my favorite nephew looks like a prince in his new kanzu," he said as he helped them bring in the food and gifts.

"Thanks, Ayaz Uncle." Tehzeeb grabbed the card he'd tucked into his sketchbook. "Look what I drew for you!"

"Asante sana! What a remarkable Navroz card. This is definitely going on the fridge."

Tehzeeb's heart glowed. He always enjoyed sharing his work with others.

"Keep it up, buddy, and remember—practice makes progress!" Ayaz Uncle said with a grin.

Tehzeeb giggled. "You mean practice makes perfect, right, Ayaz Uncle?"

"None of us are perfect, beta, but we can strive for perfection. You see—" But before he could continue, there came a shout from across the house.

"Tez! My baby cousin! Come over here and say hi to the bride-to-be!" It was Rahima!

Tehzeeb followed her voice into the living room. One wall was decorated with a flowery backdrop and the couch where Rahima was sitting had been moved in front of it. She wore a purple kurta over jeans. Beside her was an older, curly-haired lady in a green dress.

"Navroz Mubarak, kiddo," Rahima said. "This is Jenny Bai. She's going to be doing my mehndi for my wedding later this year. She's the most famous mehndi artist in town." Tehzeeb's eyes widened—the most famous mehndi artist? He just *had* to see her designs!

"Would you like me to apply some henna on you, beta?" Jenny Bai said with a twinkle in her eye. "I need to show your cousin some of my most special designs so she can decide which one she wants on her wedding day."

Tehzeeb didn't even have to think about it. "Yes!" he answered excitedly.

He'd seen women wear these splendid designs at weddings, Eids, Khushialis, and other celebrations, but no one had ever asked if he'd like any. Well, not until today.

"Wonderful! Let's get started."

Tehzeeb rolled up his sleeve and held out his left palm.

Jenny Bai snipped the top of a mehndi cone and then pointed the tip against his skin. Gently, she spread the lines of a greenish-brown paste and made a small dot in the middle of his palm. It reminded Tehzeeb of cake icing—only this didn't look as tasty.

"It tickles," laughed Tehzeeb. "And it smells like . . . like nothing I've ever smelled before. But I love it."

"You're smelling the spice of clove and the mintiness of eucalyptus," Jenny Bai said with a chuckle. She then began adding petals to the dot . . . and suddenly the dot had become a flower.

Tehzeeb tried to stay as still as a sculpture. He watched as she delicately drew daffodils and daisies, painted perfectly teardrop-shaped paisleys, checkered diamonds along his fingers, and filled every last space with vines, squiggles, and the coolest complicated patterns.

Before he knew it, she had covered his hand with a glamorous garden—a garden that reminded him of the Navroz card he'd made on the car ride there.

Tezheeb's heart danced. He had always loved drawing designs in his sketchbook, but now, it was as if his hands were the paper, and the more he stared at his palm, he could almost feel it come to life! He knew he had to try it for himself. But he'd only ever drawn with pencil crayons and markers before.

"Thank you so much, Jenny Bai!"

"You are most welcome, beta," she said with a smile. "Now, you must remember: you need to wait till it dries completely before flaking the paste off. If not, it will smudge and ruin the design. And the longer you keep it, the darker the mehndi stain will become."

Tezheeb found a quiet spot away from everyone and stared at his hand, waiting for the paste to dry. He noticed it was starting to harden slowly and blew on his hand. But it was taking so long! Everyone had already begun eating chocolate cake and sipping pink sherbet, but he wasn't interested in

dessert. All he wanted was to make sure the mehndi dried perfectly—he didn't want to ruin Jenny Bai's beautiful artwork.

As his family finished dessert and began saying their goodbyes, Jenny Bai walked over and slid a brand-new cone into Tehzeeb's backpack.

"I saw how closely you watched me do your mehndi. I also noticed the Navroz card your Ayaz Uncle put on the fridge. You're very artistic. Why not give mehndi a try, beta?" she said with a wink.

Chapter 3

On the car ride home, Tehzeeb could only think of the brand-new cone Jenny Bai had given him. It was like she'd read his mind!

He wanted to make a design just like the one Jenny Bai had done for him. He could picture exactly what he wanted to draw: a bouquet of roses, a palace fit for

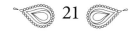

a prince, and a bunch of clouds with the sun peeking through. Maybe even Mr. Unicorn, too.

"Mom, could I practice some mehndi on you?" asked Tehzeeb once they got home and he had finished flaking off his own mehndi and changing out of his kanzu.

"I'd love that. When I was a little girl back in Tanzania, my friends practiced their designs on me all the time. And did you know Jenny Bai did my wedding mehndi?" She rolled up her sleeve and held out her arm to Tehzeeb.

He felt a rush of excitement down his back. He was getting to practice mehndi for the first time! His eyes widened as he stared at his mom's arm. It was like staring at a blank page. *Hmmm. Where should I begin?* His head was flooded with ideas.

Trying to stay as steady as he could, he drew a dot the size of a pea on his mom's hand. But his pea was more of an oval than a circle.

Maybe I just need to smooth the edges, he thought. But when he tried to fix it, the circle just grew bigger, and bigger, and bigger . . . Soon, his pea was as big as a cucumber slice. What was he going to do?

"Ugh, now I have to start all over again," he said, grabbing a paper towel to wipe the paste off. "I'm sorry, Mom. I guess I am just not as good as Jenny Bai."

"Oh no, Tehzeeb. Please finish what you've started. Even Jenny Bai had to start somewhere. You're doing great!"

His mom had a point. He had just started and couldn't give up quite yet. Thinking about Jenny Bai gave him an idea. He remembered what she had done when she first applied his mehndi. She added petals to her dot . . . maybe he could do that, too!

Soon enough, Tehzeeb had transformed his blob into something familiar. He had created a sunflower on his mom's palm! He carefully painted her fingertips and added a few finishing swirls. It was simple, but he felt like it was done.

"Wow, Tehzeeb, this reminds me of the famous mehndi designs that Bollywood actresses get in the movies," his mom exclaimed.

Tehzeeb felt relieved. He was glad he had made

his mom happy. But he was also disappointed he couldn't bring his imagination to life with mehndi as easily as he could when he was drawing in his sketchbook.

Then he remembered what Ayaz Uncle had told him. *Practice makes progress.*

Tehzeeb spent the rest of the night doodling dots, lines, squiggles, and shapes on the back of his palm. Maybe, just maybe, he could be as good as Jenny Bai one day.

Chapter 4

Tehzeeb could not get mehndi off his mind. At school, he doodled designs in his notebook during class. At lunch, he found a shady spot under a tree to try to bring those designs to life.

It didn't take long for his friends to notice.

"Can you do some henna on me? Pretty please!"

asked his best friend Maya.

"Okay, but I only know how to do simple ones," he told her, choosing only to draw another sunflower and to write her name. He was excited to practice mehndi on his friends, but he didn't want to disappoint them if the design did not come out as planned.

But Maya was so thrilled to have a mehndi design—even if it was a simple one. She told everyone she knew, and before long, almost all the kids in his grade wanted some.

Not everyone was positive, though. Safa pinched her nose and yelled, "Ewww, that's stinky!" when she smelled the mehndi. Tehzeeb's reading buddy, Jason,

laughed at him and called the mehndi "poop."

But Tehzeeb didn't let those mean kids stop him. He was proud of his unique art form, even if it was different than what they were used to. Over the next few days, he practiced on his classmates and even drew a design on his teacher's wrist. When he ran out of mehndi, his mom was able to buy more cones at the Indian grocery store. Soon enough, everybody at school had a new nickname for him: Mehndi Boy.

As the weeks passed, his hand grew steadier and he came up with even more creative designs. But no matter how good he got, he still made mistakes. His heart would break every time he smudged his work or squirted mehndi where he didn't mean for it to go.

He knew the mehndi would fade in a week or so, but most days, his mistakes made him feel terrible. He didn't want to upset the people who were so eager to let him practice on them. Even though they usually didn't say anything mean, he could tell they were disappointed when he didn't get it right.

If he ever wanted to be as good as Jenny Bai, he would have to learn to not make mistakes. Bridal mehndi had to be *perfect* on the first try.

Practice makes progress, he kept telling himself. Even if it didn't always feel that way.

When school let out for the summer, Tehzeeb brought his mehndi cone in his backpack everywhere he went. He practiced on anyone who'd lend him their hand, arm, or wrist. He applied mehndi to his neighbor Mrs. Singh, who was excited to see Tehzeeb practicing on his porch. She was so thrilled she gifted him a bag of fresh chilies from her garden. He made a butterfly for Ms. Baxter, the curious librarian at his public library, who was surprised to see the beautiful henna on his hands. He even practiced on his little cousins, twins Adam and Alisha, when they came over for a sleepover.

Even when he was alone, he'd still end up doodling all over his hand, testing out the harder techniques, styles, and shapes on himself before doing them on others. Tehzeeb's hands were always covered with the most unusual and unique patterns.

Soon, his simple designs became more intricate— marvelous marigolds, dazzling daisies, and regal roses fit for a botanical garden. He drew arches and domes that reminded him of medieval castles and majestic mosques. He drew curvy clouds, grand galaxies, squirmy squiggles, and delicate dots. He made charming checkerboard and even perfected paisleys. Tehzeeb's practice was finally paying off.

Every time he did a new design, he felt like he was in training, each time getting closer and closer to his goal of becoming as talented and famous as Jenny Bai one day. He imagined the exquisite designs he would create for all the brides in town and all the weddings he'd be invited to. All the aunties would know his name and all the brides would want Mehndi Boy to do their mehndi on their big day.

For now, though, he would need to be happy with doing his own mehndi and his mom's in time for Rahima's wedding. It might not be bridal mehndi, but Tehzeeb would make sure it was as perfect as possible. If he wasn't doing mehndi for the bride, at least he could make their mehndi look fit for a bride! He couldn't wait to show Ayaz Uncle and the rest of the family the progress he'd made.

Chapter 5

It was finally the week before Rahima's wedding. Tehzeeb's family went over to Ayaz Uncle's house to help prepare the decorations. Tehzeeb was so excited for his cousin's big day.

His aunties complimented him as he helped them arrange centerpieces.

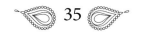

"Wow! You did that henna yourself?" said Parin Mami.

"What a unique design!" exclaimed Fatima Masi.

"You must do my mehndi next week, beta. Jenny Bai, you've taught him well," announced Naz Bai.

"I'm afraid I can't take any credit," Jenny Bai replied. "Tez learned this all by himself!"

Tehzeeb glowed with all the compliments. His uncle walked over as Jenny Bai was admiring his palm up close.

"Ayaz Uncle, look at my hands!" Tehzeeb said as he bounced on his toes. "I've been practicing every day since Navroz. Do you want me to do a little design on your palm for the wedding next week?"

Ayaz Uncle's face grew cold. Tehzeeb felt the hairs stand up on the back of his neck.

"Tehzeeb, mehndi is for girls and ladies. Boys don't wear mehndi. Boys don't do mehndi. It's just . . . it's just . . . wrong," he mumbled before storming away.

Tehzeeb's heart started drumming like a dhol. *Dhuk dhuk dhuk.* His hands were sweating. He could feel himself shrinking and his world growing colder. What just happened? How could mehndi be wrong? How could something so beautiful be wrong?

"Tehzeeb, your uncle doesn't understand you, but that shouldn't stop you," Jenny Bai said after some silence. "In India, many men are skillful henna artists and many grooms even do mehndi on their big day, too. You're doing wonderfully. You keep on doing what you're doing, beta."

Jenny Bai's kind words helped a little, but Tehzeeb still felt like crying. He buried his face in his hands.

"Tez, what's wrong?" He looked up to see Rahima rushing over. He could only shrug.

"Awww, baby cuz. I hate seeing you upset. But I promise you, whatever it is, it'll get better." He couldn't stop a tear from escaping. Rahima put an arm around his shoulders. "Would you like to ride in the limousine with me next week on the way to the pithi ceremony?"

Tehzeeb nodded, trying to smile. He had never ridden in a limousine before, but as happy as he was

40

about it, he just couldn't seem to push Ayaz Uncle's words out of his head. He felt like someone had replaced his heart with a stone.

His favorite uncle did not approve of his talent, even though so many other people did. Was he not a boy? Or not the *right* kind of boy? How could something that brought him—and others—so much happiness upset his uncle? What Ayaz Uncle said didn't make sense to Tehzeeb, but it did hurt him. Should he stop doing mehndi so that his uncle would like him again? So he could be Ayaz Uncle's favorite nephew again? Giving up mehndi would mean he would never get to see his friends' faces light up or get to imagine any more creative designs ever again.

The rest of the day passed in a blur. Tezheeb couldn't stop thinking about his uncle's words. But thinking about giving up mehndi made him feel like his world would be drained of color and happiness.

Chapter 6

It was the day of Rahima's pithi ceremony, and Tehzeeb was supposed to be getting ready. Instead, he was lying glumly on his bed, staring at the ceiling.

He hadn't touched his mehndi cones all week. For the first time in months, they'd stayed tucked away in his drawer. The pattern he'd made on his hand the week before had faded away, since Tehzeeb had used extra soap on it every day.

Each time he looked at his cones, he remembered what Ayaz Uncle had said, and it confused him more and more. Tehzeeb knew that Ayaz Uncle understood him, and it wasn't just because of the kanzu and all the other unique souvenirs from his travels. In the past, Ayaz Uncle had always given him the best advice. Tehzeeb could usually trust whatever his uncle thought was best. But somehow, things changed when it came to mehndi. Tehzeeb wanted to follow his uncle's advice, but it just didn't make sense to him. How was mehndi different from any other kind of art?

Every time he thought about it, his heart pounded

and his tummy felt sick. Maybe Ayaz Uncle was right after all. Maybe mehndi just wasn't for boys. Maybe Tehzeeb would be better off without it.

As excited as he was to ride in the limousine with Rahima, he was scared to see Ayaz Uncle again. He couldn't stop picturing his uncle's look of disappointment last week. Did he still like Tehzeeb or was he upset with him? Was he still his uncle's favorite nephew? All these questions gave Tehzeeb a headache.

"Tez, we're leaving in five minutes!" his mom called out.

Oh no! Tehzeeb shot up, untying the towel turbaned around his long-dried hair.

Tehzeeb rushed around his room, collecting the

different parts of his outfit. Even though he was feeling down, he couldn't help but smile when he spotted his jeweled burgundy kurta in his closet.

Tehzeeb dove into the kurta. It glimmered like a ruby in the rays of the afternoon sun shining into his bedroom. Instantly, he felt so handsome and confident. In that moment, Tehzeeb felt like he was serving the world a piece of cake of who he was inside—the creative and imaginative Tez. He felt like he was exactly who he wanted to be. Well, almost . . .

Something—the cherry on top—was missing.

But Tehzeeb didn't have time to think about that. He hurried to fill his backpack with a change of clothes, his sketchbook, and, of course, Mr. Unicorn.

As he reached for his pencil crayons, he noticed his mehndi cones in the back of the drawer.

He hesitated. He remembered how badly he wanted to do mehndi for his mom and himself. But then he thought about what Ayaz Uncle had said. At the last second, he tossed a cone into his bag. It was the cherry on top. Like having Mr. Unicorn in his backpack, carrying the mehndi cone just felt right, even if he wasn't going to take it out today.

"Tehzeeb! Let's go. I don't want you to miss the limousine," his mom called out again. He raced downstairs to fill his water bottle and add some snacks to his backpack. He found his mom wearing a classic mustard-colored bhandani sari. His dad wore a gray suit with a matching mustard-colored tie and handkerchief. Tehzeeb hated dull gray suits—he was excited he'd get to glow like a ruby in his kurta.

On the way to Rahima's place, Tehzeeb's nervous–ness grew and grew. Butterflies did somersaults in his stomach as they arrived. His heart thumped like a dhol when he knocked on the door. *Dhuk dhuk dhuk.*

As the door swung open, Tehzeeb's jaw dropped.

"Tez! You're just in time," announced Rahima. He was stunned to see his cousin dressed like a princess in a teal ghagra choli. It had gorgeous golden vines along the skirt and fancy frills on the blouse. "Every-one else is already at the hall, so it's just us and my bridesmaids. The limo should be here any minute."

Ayaz Uncle wasn't even here? *Phew.* Now he could finally enjoy the limousine ride.

Rahima's bridesmaids were quick to welcome Tehzeeb. They complimented his kurta, and one of them, Raisa, even gave Tehzeeb a magnificent matching scarf to wear with his outfit.

A few minutes later, a shiny white limousine rolled up the driveway, and they all piled inside.

The ceiling of the limousine looked like a disco ball, with bright colors moving around like the Northern Lights. It was the coolest thing he'd ever seen! Rahima's friends danced to their favorite rap

and hip hop tracks as they drove toward the banquet hall.

They'd barely made it a few blocks before the limousine came to a halt. "It seems we've hit a bit of traffic, ladies," called out the driver.

"Don't worry, it shouldn't take long," said Raisa.

"It'll clear up in no time," said another bridesmaid.

But when Tehzeeb peered out the window, he saw a looooong lineup of cars in front of them—an ocean of red lights as far as he could see. His cousin began tapping her leg and frantically looking out the window.

"Rahima, everything will be okay," he said, trying to comfort her.

Five minutes turned into twenty-five minutes and then an hour. Rahima's cell phone rang. It was Ayaz Uncle. The guests had arrived, the food was soon to be served, and the most important person of the pithi—the bride—was still stuck in traffic!

Worst of all, Jenny Bai had another wedding to get to and would need to leave the banquet hall soon. Who would do Rahima's mehndi now?

Chapter 7

Rahima started to cry. As much as she didn't care for the smell of mehndi paste, Tehzeeb knew she definitely wanted to fulfill the tradition in time for her wedding.

Should I ask her if she wants me to do her mehndi? he wondered. *No, I don't want to upset Ayaz Uncle.*

He handed his cousin the water bottle from his backpack. "Take a sip. I promise everything will work out okay!"

"Thanks, Tez," she said, still sniffing.

As Tehzeeb zipped up his bag, the mehndi cone fell to the floor.

"Tez!" exclaimed Rahima. "You could do my mehndi in the limousine!"

Tehzeeb felt his heart lurch—he wanted so badly to jump up and say yes. But he couldn't stop thinking of everything Ayaz Uncle had said. Mehndi wasn't something boys should do . . . right?

"Are you sure, Rahima?" he asked, nervous butterflies churning in his stomach.

"Please, baby cuz. What is everyone going to say if they see my hands and feet undecorated? What about all the pictures? I've seen your work—it's fabulous. Please?" she repeated, tears welling in her eyes.

"Okay . . . I'll try my best," said Tehzeeb as confidently as he could. Now his nervousness felt like a volcano, but he reminded himself that his cousin needed him.

Rahima's eyes lit up. She let out a huge sigh of relief. "Yes, baby cuz! Please do a design on me—any design!" Her bridesmaids cheered for Tehzeeb.

His hands shaky, Tehzeeb put the cone to her hand and paused.

Am I really doing bridal henna right now? he thought. *What have I gotten myself into?*

When he'd said he wanted to be like Jenny Bai, he hadn't realized it would be like this. He hadn't realized it would be so soon! Had he practiced enough? What should he draw for his cousin?

Tehzeeb took a deep breath. He'd have to move these questions to the back of his mind. Right now, he had to focus on the most important task: creating mehndi fit for a bride.

He painted patterns with paisleys, laid lavish lace across her wrist, formed fancy florals, patterned proud pretty peacocks, and drew detailed domes that reminded him of the Taj Mahal. Before he knew it, he had covered her hand with a dazzling scene. He could almost feel it come to life in her palm.

As he was applying the last swirl, the limousine jerked forward—they weren't stuck in the traffic jam anymore! But the jerk caused him to squirt a big squiggle on Rahima's hand. *Oh no!* Tehzeeb started sweating and his head spun.

What was he going to do to fix this? He had to make it perfect—it was bridal mehndi after all. *I've fixed mistakes before,* he reminded himself, like when he practiced the first time with his mom. His heart raced. How was he going to fix this one?

Tehzeeb's eyes landed on the glorious golden vines embroidered on the skirt of Rahima's ghagra choli.

Hmmm . . .

He looked back at the squiggle. It did kind of curve

like a vine . . .

Maybe this wasn't a mistake after all! he thought.

Tehzeeb carefully drew leaves and jasmine flowers

along the squiggle. Soon, the mistake had transformed

into a vine—a perfect match to the one on her skirt.

As cautiously as he could, he worked on her other hand as the limousine raced on. He had to be careful every time they hit a bump to make sure the mehndi was fit for his favorite cousin's big day.

He decorated every inch of Rahima's hands, using every last ounce of his mehndi. He was done!

"Look, Rahima! It's finally perf—"

Before Tehzeeb could complete his thought, the car braked suddenly. Tehzeeb lost his balance. He smeared his hand across Rahima's left palm, smudging the design he'd worked so hard on.

"Noooooo!" he cried.

Just like that, his perfect masterpiece was now imperfect.

Chapter 8

"I've ruined everything, Rahima. I'm so sorry," Tezheeb said quietly. "I was trying to be so careful. I am the worst." He looked away, too upset to face his cousin.

All the feelings he thought he had tucked away came flooding back. *"Boys don't wear mehndi. Boys*

don't do mehndi." Ayaz Uncle's disapproving face kept popping into his mind. A boy doing mehndi was one thing. A boy doing *imperfect* mehndi—that was way worse.

And what about his poor cousin? He had ruined her big day! He kept imagining her angry and disappointed face until finally he felt a soft hand on his shoulder.

He made himself turn around. But instead of anger, he saw kindness in Rahima's eyes and a smile on her red lips.

"Awww, you're not the worst, Tez. Don't worry at all, baby cuz. The car braking was out of your control. The other hand is amazing, and so what if this hand got a bit smudged?"

Rahima's kindness helped a little, but Tehzeeb was still upset. "It's not just you," he said.

Rahima frowned. "What do you mean?"

He took a deep breath. Should he tell Rahima about Ayaz Uncle? He didn't want her to feel bad on the day of her pithi ceremony, but he had to get it off his chest. "I'm really nervous about what Ayaz Uncle will say. He doesn't like that I do mehndi. He says

it's wrong for a boy to do it. I'm worried he'll be even more upset with me since I ruined your design."

"Awww, Tez. I get it. Dad is very open-minded about a lot of things, but there are still some things he is a bit old-fashioned about. Remember, he's an artist just like you. He'll come around soon enough." She gave him a tight hug. "Don't worry, though. I've got your back! You saved my big day, and I'll make sure no one bothers you."

Tehzeeb hugged his cousin back. But he was still uneasy.

Chapter 9

"You made it!" Jenny Bai called out when they finally pulled up to the banquet hall. She had been waiting for them outside the main entrance.

She looked at Rahima's hands in surprise then turned to Tehzeeb.

He froze. What would the most famous mehndi

artist in town think of his work?

"*Shukar Mawla!* Wow, Tez, you did a wonderful job on her hands."

The butterflies in Tehzeeb's tummy eased up a bit. He was so honored and relieved that Jenny Bai liked what he had done.

"Rahima, since I have to leave in fifteen minutes, can I have Tehzeeb help me finish applying mehndi to your feet?" asked Jenny Bai.

"I wouldn't have it any other way!" Rahima replied with a smile.

All the guests watched in awe as they made their grand entrance. Rahima got to sit on a fancy chair in the middle of the stage, and it reminded Tehzeeb

of a throne. Both Jenny Bai and Tehzeeb sat on the ground by Rahima's legs and began working on the mehndi on her feet. He could hear the excitement and the chatter from the crowd.

"Jenny Bai isn't doing her mehndi alone?"

"A little boy is helping her do Rahima's mehndi?"

"Wow, look at the beautiful design he is doing. He's so talented!"

Tehzeeb blurred out all the voices. He was focused on doing a good job on Rahima's feet. From behind him, he heard a creak as someone came up the steps to the stage.

Tehzeeb turned his head and saw Ayaz Uncle walking over with a colorful tray in his hands. *Dhuk*

dhuk dhuk. His heart began banging like a dhol again—he wished he could hide in a corner. He didn't want to disappoint his uncle more than he already had.

"Wah, Jenny Bai, did you do this all right now?" Ayaz Uncle said in amazement.

"No, Ayaz Bha. Tehzeeb did this on the ride here. This is the handiwork of your nephew," she said proudly.

There was a long pause. "Dad, don't you have anything to say about Tez's amazing work?" asked Rahima.

"The designs are very nice, and they look beautiful on her. Thank you," Tehzeeb's uncle said eventually. He stared down at the tray he was holding.

For some reason, his uncle's compliment didn't make Tehzeeb feel any better. He knew more needed to be said, but he felt frozen.

"It really is the most stunning mehndi I've ever had. Thanks, Tez," Rahima said before turning back to her father. "Dad, is it time for the pithi ceremony yet?"

"Right! Let's get some haidar on you now," said Ayaz Uncle. He slipped a small chocolate into her mouth and then scooped his fingers into a bowl of orange paste on his tray. He gently smeared it on her arm.

"Tehzeeb beta, your turn!" whispered Ayaz Uncle as he lowered the tray. Tehzeeb gulped. He fed his cousin another chocolate and then plopped some of the orange paste onto her nose. They both giggled.

"Go grab some food, beta, you must be tired," said Ayaz Uncle, giving him a pat on the back.

Tehzeeb was glad that his uncle appreciated his work and was acting normally again. But the food just didn't taste as yummy . . . Something still didn't quite feel right. Did this mean Ayaz Uncle was okay with him doing mehndi? Was he still upset with him? Was Tehzeeb still his favorite nephew? He was just too tired to think about it. His mind had raced enough today.

Raisa and the rest of the bridesmaids pulled him into the middle of the raas where they twirled in a circle, all swaying to the same dance moves. As Tehzeeb danced to the beat of the dhol, the nervous dhol inside of him got quieter. After a whole week of worrying what people would think, he finally felt at peace. He realized that he knew exactly what made him Tez, what made him himself: his creativity. What he wanted most was to hug that happiness and never let it go.

Later that evening, when Rahima and Tehzeeb struck dandiya sticks, he spotted his uncle across the dance floor. Tehzeeb swallowed. The dhol inside him thumped a little louder. He knew he needed to tell his uncle how he felt. But he didn't want to be scared or upset again tonight. He'd talk to Ayaz Uncle tomorrow at the nikah.

For the rest of the night, Tehzeeb danced with the new friends he'd made in the limousine, feeling nothing but freedom.

Chapter 10

After a long night of food, celebration, and trying not to think about what he still needed to tell his uncle, Tehzeeb was exhausted. But he and his family had to wake up bright and early to head to the Jamatkhana where the nikah was taking place. The day of Rahima's marriage ceremony had finally arrived!

As soon as he saw Rahima enter the prayer hall, Tehzeeb's sleepiness went away. She looked gorgeous in her snow-white bridal sari, the sweetest smelling jasmine in her hair, and the majestic dark red stain of her mehndi on her hands, arms, and feet. If he squinted, he could still see the smudge on her left palm. He hoped she wasn't disappointed and that the guests would pay more attention to her stunning outfit and bright smile. Her fiancé, Karim, looked dashing in a white sherwani and a cream-colored shawl with a pretty paisley pattern. They wore matching pearl tasbihs on their right wrists that shimmered as they made their way to the front of the hall to meet with the Mukhi Saheb conducting the ceremony.

Even though he'd made a mistake, Tehzeeb was thrilled he could help Rahima be the princess she was on her big day. Since he'd gotten his first mehndi cone, he had made so many new friends, shared his art with his neighbors, classmates, and family—and even got to do bridal mehndi just like Jenny Bai. He *loved* doing mehndi. It made him feel like his true creative self.

And still, thinking about the disappointment in Ayaz Uncle's eyes and the things he had said made him feel small and ashamed.

Tehzeeb tried to push his worries about his uncle out of his mind while he listened to the Quranic recitations and watched his cousin sign the marriage contract.

Before he knew it, the bride and groom were wed! He cheered along with the crowd and joined the long line to congratulate Rahima and her new husband.

While guests enjoyed the beef sambusas and the masala chai served in the social hall, Tehzeeb saw his chance to take care of the one thing that was still weighing on his heart: Ayaz Uncle.

When Ayaz Uncle finally had a break from guests congratulating him, Tehzeeb snuck up behind him and tapped his shoulder.

"Oh, Tehzeeb beta!" he said as he turned around.

Tehzeeb still didn't really know what to say, but he just knew he had to say *something*. "Mubaraki, Ayaz Uncle. I—"

"Thank you, beta, Mubaraki!" his uncle cut in. "I wanted to speak to you, too. Is it okay if I go first?"

Tehzeeb nodded nervously, his heart thumping. *Dhuk dhuk dhuk.*

"I did some thinking last night, and I just wanted to say sorry." He let out a small sigh. "I am sorry for telling you that boys shouldn't wear or do mehndi. You've shown me your commitment to your craft. You've worked so hard and your designs look amazing on Rahima."

Tehzeeb's eyes filled with tears. "But Ayaz Uncle, I smudged her palm," he said. "I thought you were going to be super mad at me. Not just for that but because I was doing mehndi in the first place."

Ayaz Uncle took a long look at Tehzeeb.

"Beta, I am not mad at you about smudging her

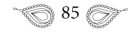

mehndi. You did your best, and we are all still very grateful. Remember, practice is not about perfection, it is about progress."

"Can I tell you something?" asked Tehzeeb. He took a deep breath. He finally felt like he could say what was on his mind.

"Of course, beta."

"Instead of using my pencil crayons to doodle something on paper where it's stuck in my sketchbook forever, I want to use mehndi to share my imagination with everyone. It makes me happy when I make others happy. It doesn't matter if I do my art in sketchbooks or on my friends' hands, or even my own hand, it's still my art. Even if I am a boy—so what?"

Ayaz Uncle nodded. "I made a mistake. I am sorry for making you feel like you shouldn't do mehndi. Mehndi is for everyone, just like art is for everyone. All my life, I have been used to certain roles and traditions for men and women, but you're challenging me to look beyond it." He put his hand on Tehzeeb's shoulder. "I can't say I will get it right all the time, but I promise I'll try."

Tehzeeb grinned. "Practice makes progress, *right*, Ayaz Uncle?"

"Right! You've taught your old uncle a lesson. I want you to always do your art, no matter what anyone says," he said with a proud look.

The last of the butterflies escaped from Tehzeeb's

tummy. His heart no longer banged like a dhol. And he felt confident. He could be himself and his uncle would be there to support him.

"Now, my favorite nephew, when is it going to be my turn to get some mehndi?"

Tehzeeb smiled as he reached for the cone in his back pocket. "I thought you'd never ask!"

Glossary

Acho, acho! Andar acho! is a Kutchi phrase that translates to "Come, come! Come inside!"

Asante sana means "thank you very much" in Swahili.

Bai means "sister" in Kutchi and is often used as a term of respect when referring to older women. **Bha** means "brother" in Kutchi and is often used as a term of respect when referring to older men.

Beta means "son" but can be used by elders more generally to refer to a young person.

Bhandani is a tie-dye cloth used to make scarves, saris, and more. It is traditionally made in Gujarat and other areas of India.

Channa bateta is a tangy chickpea and potato curry cooked in a spiced tomato gravy. It is a beloved fusion East African-Indian dish and is often served with a drizzle of tamarind chutney and garnished with potato chips.

Dandiya is a folk dance originating in Kutch and Gujarat. Each person holds a bamboo stick and hits their dance partner's stick in time to the beat. **Raas** is another popular folk dance where everyone does similar moves as they dance in a line or in a circle.

Dhol is a double-headed drum used in festivals and celebrations throughout South Asia.

Eid is the Arabic word for "feast" or "festival" and refers to the significant holy days that are celebrated by Muslims.

Ghagra choli is a festive garment made up of a cropped blouse and flowing skirt, often paired with a scarf.

Haidar means "turmeric" in Kutchi.

Jamatkhana serves as the place of worship and community center for Ismaili Muslims.

Kanzu is an ankle-length tunic that serves as a traditional garment worn in East Africa. Tanzanian kanzus have a distinctive tassel that hangs from their collar, and they are often worn with a cylindrical kofia hat.

Khushiali refers to festival days that are celebrated specifically by Ismaili Muslims.

Kurta is a traditional loose-fitting tunic made out of either cotton or silk, often embroidered with designs. It is worn by both men and women in South Asia.

Mandazi, also known as mahamri or African doughnuts, are sweet fried buns that originate from the coastal region of East Africa.

Mubaraki is an expression used whenever congratulations are due in Kutchi.

Mukhi Saheb refers to the head of a particular Jamatkhana, who leads daily rituals and represents the Imam of the Time. For Ismaili Muslims, the Imam is a spiritual leader from the family of Prophet Muhammad who offers spiritual and material guidance.

Navroz (or Nowruz) is the Persian New Year and first day of spring celebrated by Persian, Central Asian, and some South Asian communities as well as the Bahai, Ismaili, and Zoroastrian religious communities. **Navroz Mubarak** is used by South Asians to wish others a happy Navroz.

Nikah is an Islamic marriage ceremony.

Pithi is a pre-wedding ceremony. There are usually separate pithi ceremonies for the bride and groom. Often, turmeric pastes and mehndi are applied to the bride by loved ones.

Quranic means something relating to the Qur'an, the Muslim holy book.

Roji, also known as sabzeh, is a wheatgrass traditionally grown before Navroz to mark the beginning of spring.

Sambusa is the Swahili term for a popular fried pastry with a savory filling also known as samosa in South Asia.

Sari is a traditional garment worn by women across South Asia that consists of a blouse and a long piece of fabric that is draped several times around the body.

Sherwani is an outfit popularly worn at formal events such as weddings by North Indian men and is of Turkish and Persian origin.

Sherbet is a celebratory drink made by combining milk, rose syrup, and ice cream.

Shukar Mawla is an expression that means "Thank God" in Kutchi.

Topi means "hat" in Kutchi.

Wah is a Hindi expression that means "wow" or "bravo."

Ya Ali Madad is the greeting used by Ismaili Muslims when they meet one another. It translates to "May Ali help you." **Mawla Ali Madad** is the response greeting, and it translates to "May Ali help you too."

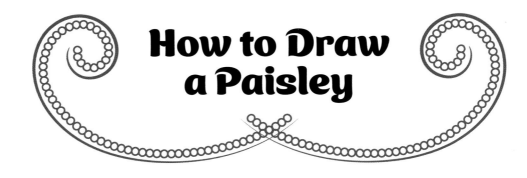

How to Draw a Paisley

Paisley designs are a regal yet simple pattern often used in mehndi art. A paisley, or boteh in Farsi, is a teardrop-shaped symbol with a curved upper end. It is said to represent a cypress tree. Originally a design in textiles like Kashmiri shawls, the popularity of these shawls in Europe means paisley designs can be found on English silk ties, too. Follow these steps to draw your own paisley pattern!

1. Begin by drawing a backward S-shaped curve. One side of the curve should be smaller than the other.

2. Draw a small teardrop shape at the end of the smaller part of the curve.

3. Draw a curved line that connects the top of the smaller part of the S to the larger end of it. That will close the shape and form your paisley.

4. Decorate the inside of your paisley with different lines, shading, dots, and shapes. You can copy the flower design inside the paisley on the next page or make up your own patterns!

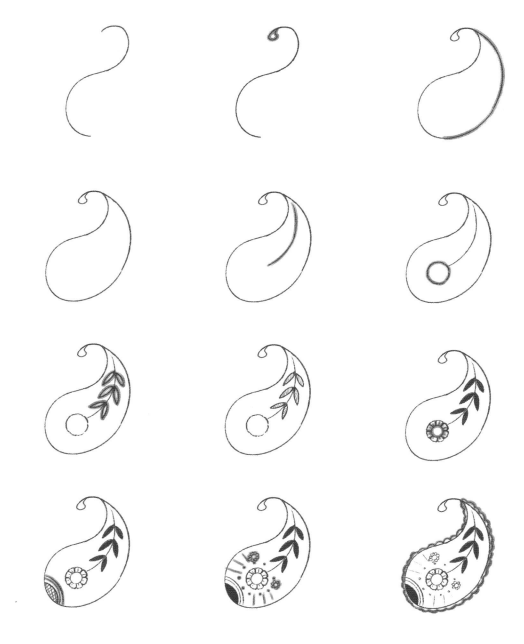

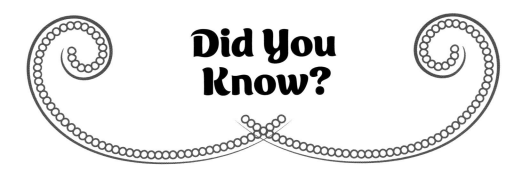

Did You Know?

- Ancient Egypt was the first recorded place where henna was used. It was commonly applied on skin, hair, and nails. In fact, the mummy of Pharaoh Ramesses II was found with his hair stained a red-orange color that has survived to this day!

- Henna comes from a plant called *Lawsonia inermis*, also known as the henna tree. The leaves are collected, dried, milled, and sifted into a powder. The powder is combined with liquids like tea, water, lemon juice, and essential oils to create a paste.

- While using a plastic cone to apply detailed henna patterns is the most common way to use it today, that wasn't always the case! In the past, the paste would have been smeared on the palm, completely covering it in a solid wash of color. Sometimes a small stick was used to move the paste around to form simple designs.

In North India, a popular tradition for bridal mehndi is to hide the groom's initials or name within the bride's mehndi pattern. The newlywed couple can then have fun trying to find the name during their wedding night.

The word "mehndi" comes from the root word "mendhikā" in Sanskrit, meaning "which gives color." The term "henna" comes from the Arabic term "al-ḥinnā," which refers to the henna plant itself.

Henna as a body art tradition is practiced across the globe. Regions like South Asia, North Africa, East Africa, and the Middle East all have distinct styles and techniques, and these communities have brought these practices wherever they have migrated around the world.

Acknowledgments

A friend and I were once lost in Berlin, trying to find a Jamatkhana, an Ismaili place of worship, so that we could attend Friday prayers. It was dark, and we were in an unfamiliar place as immature exchange students. We weren't alone though. Turns out, another boy our age was also lost, trying to find it, and he was a student studying abroad like us. We ended up grabbing a bite together and becoming friends that evening. Our homesick butterflies fluttered away and we felt at home. The boy's name was Tehzeeb. I told myself I'd name my child Tehzeeb one day. And I did, in a way.

As a debut author, believing in myself was one of the hardest things I've ever had to do. I've learned it is a constant process, it takes reminders, and it takes community. Thank you to the supporters in my life who have held me when I felt I wasn't enough, for reminding me that my words hold power and that my creativity deserves to be shared.

I have immense gratitude for Claire Caldwell, who saw the potential in *Mehndi Boy* when it was just an outline submitted to the Annick Press Mentorship Program—a program designed to support writers from groups historically excluded from children's publishing in North America. Her empathy and communication made me feel so cared for and understood—all parts of me. To Jani Balakumar, I simply will never be able to fully express the gratitude I have for you. Your magical illustrations are everything and more than I could have imagined. To my mentor Sheniz Janmohamed, thank you for being a rock in my journey. To my friends and family, who read early drafts of *Mehndi Boy* and held space for me when I needed advice. Finally, I would like to thank myself, the inner child inside of me who longed for a book like this. Thank you for showing up even when it was tough and for giving it your all. Thank you for being your unapologetic self.

About the Author

Photo by Arthur Mola

Like Tehzeeb, **ZAIN BANDALI** was born in Canada to Ismaili Muslim parents from Tanzania. For four generations, his family lived in East Africa, with roots tracing to the Kutch and Gujarat regions of India. Zain has never felt like he had a homeland—it feels like all these places and none of these places at once. For him, home is simply where memories are made with loved ones. He loves writing poetry, collecting shawls, taking bubble baths, and hanging out in nature. Zain loves growing vegetables but cannot always stomach the hot chili peppers he grows.

About the Illustrator

JANI BALAKUMAR loves putting diversity and South Asian representation in nearly all her artwork. Growing up in Canada she often watched cartoons and wished she could make something of her own. Having a natural magnetism to art, she made a career in animation and illustration. She enjoys 2D animation as well as doing cute character designs. In her free time you can find her trying to keep her plants alive, taking care of her shrimp aquarium, going on long walks, and, of course, drawing.